The Millvill Town

Welcome to Millvill, the quaint little town nestled in the rolling hills of the countryside. With its friendly neighbours, bustling market place, and charming city hall, it's the perfect place to call home. But don't be fooled by its small size, because there's always something exciting happening in Millvill. Whether it's the annual hot air balloon festival, the grand opening of the town's newest arcade, or the latest treasure hunting adventure, there's never a dull moment in this lively town. So come on down and join in the fun with the lovable residents of Millvill, like nine-year-old Sathvik and his mischievous friends, Eoghan, Suina, James, and Charlie.

Together, they'll take you on a wild ride filled with laughter, friendship, and of course, treasure hunting

The small town of Millville was a strange and hilarious place, especially if you were a Nine year old with an active imagination. There was the old man who always walked around with a pet alligator on a leash, causing quite a stir whenever he walked down the street.

There was the ice cream truck that played offbeat music and only served flavors like pickle and bacon. And there was the town hall, which was rumored to be haunted by the ghost of a former mayor who liked to play pranks on the town council members.

It was a funny and wonderful place to grow up, and anyone who had the chance to call Millville home was lucky indeed. Nestled in the rolling hills of the countryside, Millville was home to a cast of eccentric characters. There was Mr. Jenkins, the grumpy old man who lived next door and spent all day yelling at the neighbourhood kids to stay off his lawn. There was Mrs. Patel, the kindly old lady who ran the local bakery and always had a warm smile and a free cookie for anyone who stopped by. And there was Benny, the town troublemaker, who was always up to no good and causing chaos wherever he went..

WORLD OF SATHVIK
AND HIS FRIENDS

Dear AliMay

I hope you are enjoying the summer.
This is my favourite time of the year.
Here is some more fun for you.
Satvrik is naughty & I know him very
well. Read his story and let me know
if you want to play with him

See you soon
Ritika
May 2023

Ordering Information:
Paper Back :ISBN: 9798373761147
Hard Cover : ISBN: 9798374250114

First Edition

Dear readers,

Welcome to the comical and adventurous world of Sathvik and his friends!

I'm Naveen Kumar Maremanda, the author of this book and I'm so excited to share the tales of Sathvik and his gang with you. In this book, you'll join Sathvik and his friends as they embark on a series of adventures in their hometown of Millvill. From saving a comic book store to discovering a mythical creature and even building their own go-kart to race against rival towns, these kids never run out of things to do.

But it's not just the kids who will make you laugh, their grandpa is a retired army man and grandma is a cook who will make sure to add extra humor.

You'll also get to read the special comic book series "Hairman" which was created by the gang to save the Millvill town comic book store.

So, sit back, relax and get ready for a wild ride as you turn the pages of this book. I promise you, it will be a laugh a minute!

Warmly,

Naveen Maremanda

(Naveen Maremanda)

Table of Contents

But despite its quirks, Millville was a tight-knit community where everyone knew everyone else. The people of Millville looked out for each other and always had a good laugh, no matter what life threw their way.

In short, Millville was a place where anything was possible, and a whole lot of fun was always just around the corner.

Sathvik

Meet Sathvik, the adventurous nine-year-old from the small town of MillVill. With a mischievous twinkle in his eye and a heart full of curiosity, Sathvik is always ready for his next big adventure.

Whether he's hunting for treasure with his friends or helping out at his family's food stall, The Fork and Fingers, Sathvik is always on the go. He's a bit of a troublemaker, but his heart is always in the right place. And when he's not busy exploring the town, you can find him playing video games, collecting stamps, or fishing at the local pond. But above all, Sathvik is a loyal friend who will always stand by your side, no matter what. So if you're looking for a fun-loving companion to join you on your next great adventure, look no further than Sathvik!

Sathvik's best friends are Charlie, James, Eoghan, and siuna and together, they were always up for a good time. They loved explore the town, play pranks on each other, and come up with new and creative ways to have fun .No matter what they were doing, Sathvik and his friends always had a blast. They were a tight-knit group who supported each other and always had each other's backs. Sathvik was greatful to have such amazing friends, and he knew that he was lucky to have them in his life. He couldn't wait to see what comical adventures they would have next.

4

Eoghan

Eoghan is a funny and energetic 9 year old boy from Millvill town. He loves horses and can often be found riding his favorite pony at the local stable. Eoghan is also a big fan of sweets, especially chocolate, and can often be found with a candy bar in hand. Despite his love for sweets, Eoghan can be a bit picky when it comes to food, often insisting on eating only his favorite dishes. In his spare time, Eoghan loves to listen to country music and learn new things from the elders in town. He's a bit of a nosy kid and always wants to know what's going on in Millvill. Eoghan is well-known in town and has made many friends, both young and old..

Charlie

Charlie is the tech geek of the Nuts And Bolts gang and is always eager to learn about the latest gadgets and technology. He is also a huge fan of video games and can often be found playing the latest releases with his friends. Despite his love for technology, Charlie is also very social and is always up for a good laugh with his friends. He is Sathvik best friend and the two of them are always up to some mischief together.

James

James is always full of energy and is always ready for a new adventure. He loves solving puzzles and is always up for a challenge. In fact, he's known around town as the "Puzzle King" because of his incredible ability to solve even the most difficult puzzles. But that's not all, James is also a master at making funny noises and can always be found making his friends laugh with his silly antics. Despite his mischievous nature, James is a loyal friend and always stands by his friends through thick and thin.

Siuna

Siuna is the only girl in the Nuts and Bolts gang, but she's just as adventurous and brave as the rest of the group. She's known for her quick wit, her sharp mind, and her kind heart. she's always the one organizing the gang's adventures and coming up with new ideas for activities. She's also a bit of a planner, and she loves making lists and schedules to help keep everyone on track. Despite her love of organization, siuna is also a bit of a wild child at heart. she loves nothing more than exploring the great outdoors, getting her hands dirty, and trying out new activities. Whether it's hiking, biking, or climbing, she is always up for an adventure. She's an integral part of the Nuts and Bolts gang, and the group wouldn't be complete without her.

The Nuts & Bolts Club

Sathvik and his friends, Charlie, James, Eoghan, and siuna, were the proud members of "The Nuts & Bolts Club," a club dedicated to all things wacky and weird. They met every afternoon in the Abondend Tree house at end of the Town park , where they would invent strange contraptions, play absurd games, and tell hilarious jokes. No idea was too strange or too silly for The Nuts & Bolts Club, and they always had a blast coming up with new and creative ways to have fun. The club was a haven for mischievous kids who loved to laugh and have a good time. They were always up for an adventure, whether it was exploring a haunted house or building a giant catapult. Sathvik and his friends loved being a part of The Nuts & Bolts Club, and they couldn't wait to see what crazy ideas and antics they would come up with next. It was the best club in town, and they were proud to be a part of it.

Sathivk parents runs a family cafe in Millvill Busy Market Street. The family owned food cafe "The Forks & Fingers" was a beloved fixture in the small town of Millville. It was a cozy and inviting place, with friendly staff and delicious food that always hit the spot. But the real secret to the success of The Forks & Fingers was its secret recipes, passed down from the sathvik's grandmother. These recipes were closely guarded secrets, known only to a select few within the family. The food at The Forks & Fingers was always fresh and flavourful, with a touch of magic that made every bite taste extra special. The kids of Millvill loved to visit the food stall, especially on hot summer days when they needed a cool and refreshing treat. And the adults of Millville were equally devoted to The Forks & Fingers, always raving about the delicious food and friendly atmosphere. It was the perfect place to grab a bite to eat and catch up with friends and neighbours. All in all, The Forks & Fingers was a beloved and integral part of the small town of Millville, and everyone was grateful to have such a wonderful family-owned food stall in their midst.

House of Humor

Sathvik's house in the small town of Millville was a hilarious and chaotic place, especially with his grandparents, His grandpa was a retired veteran Army man, and he was always full of stories and practical jokes. His grandma was a master cook with a secret stash of delicious recipes that she guarded with her life. Sathvik's parents were no slouches either. They ran a family food cafe called "The Forks & Fingers," and they always had a funny story or two to tell about their customers. In short, Sathvik's house was never dull. There was always something comical happening, and Sathvik loved every minute of it. He knew that he was lucky to have such a fun and loving family, and he was grateful to call Millville his home.

Sathvik's grandpa was a retired veteran Army man, and he was a force to be reckoned with. He was tough as nails and had a mischievous twinkle in his eye that always made Sathvik giggle. Grandpa was always full of funny stories from his days in the military, and he loved nothing more than to regale Sathvik and his friends with tales of his adventures. He had a knack for making even the most mundane tasks seem like thrilling missions, and the kids were always eager to listen to his stories and learn from his wisdom. But Grandpa wasn't all talk. He was also a master of practical jokes, and he loved to play pranks on Sathvik and his friends. He was always coming up with new and creative ways to make them laugh, and Sathvik never knew what to expect when he was around. Despite his tough exterior, Grandpa had a heart of gold, and Sathvik knew that he could always count on him to be there for him, no matter what. Grandpa was the best, and Sathvik loved him to pieces.

Grandpa

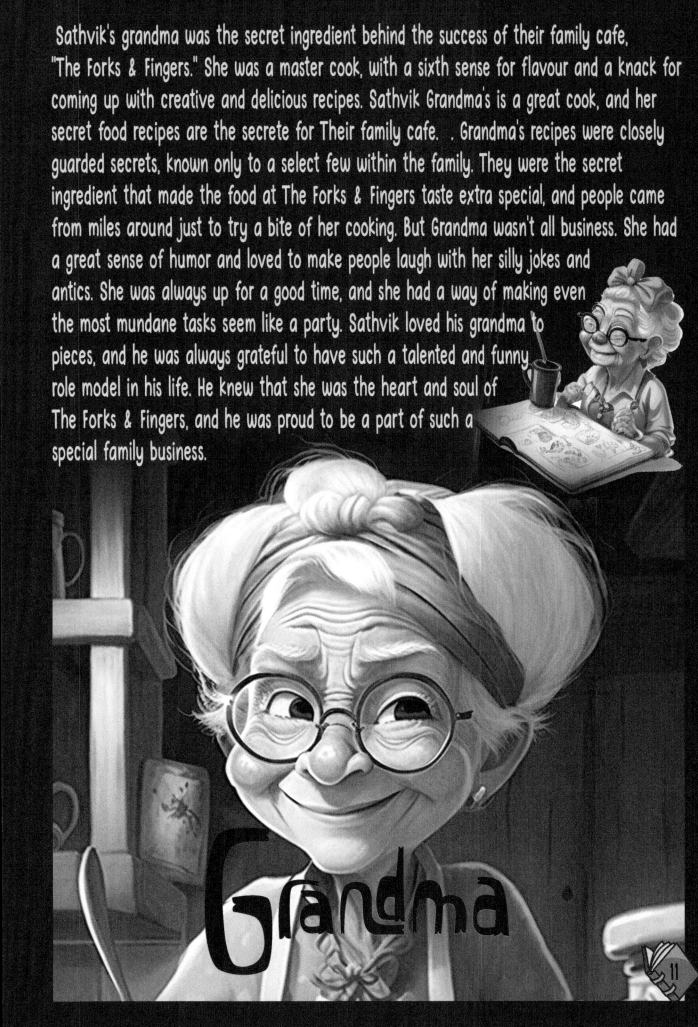

Sathvik's grandma was the secret ingredient behind the success of their family cafe, "The Forks & Fingers." She was a master cook, with a sixth sense for flavour and a knack for coming up with creative and delicious recipes. Sathvik Grandma's is a great cook, and her secret food recipes are the secrete for Their family cafe. . Grandma's recipes were closely guarded secrets, known only to a select few within the family. They were the secret ingredient that made the food at The Forks & Fingers taste extra special, and people came from miles around just to try a bite of her cooking. But Grandma wasn't all business. She had a great sense of humor and loved to make people laugh with her silly jokes and antics. She was always up for a good time, and she had a way of making even the most mundane tasks seem like a party. Sathvik loved his grandma to pieces, and he was always grateful to have such a talented and funny role model in his life. He knew that she was the heart and soul of The Forks & Fingers, and he was proud to be a part of such a special family business.

Grandma

CHAPTER I
THE ADMIRAL ARK

The Admiral's Ark

Sathivk and his friends were huge stamp collectors, and they spent hours every week adding to their collection. They had stamps from all over the world, and they loved to learn about the different countries and cultures they represented.

One day, Sathivk and his friends stumbled upon an old stamp in their collection that they had never seen before. It was a stamp from a small, mysterious island that was located just off the coast of their town, Millvill.

Sathivk: "Guys, you're not going to believe this, but I just found the rarest stamp in my collection!"

Eoghan: "What is it, a stamp from the moon or something?"

Sathivk: "Nope, it's even better. It's a stamp from a mysterious island off the coast of Millvill!"

James: "What's the island called?"

Sathivk: "It's called Lost Lagoon. And according to the stamp, it's full of hidden treasures and thrilling adventures."

12

The stamp that Sathivk found was an old, worn piece of paper with a faded image of a small, tropical island. It was roughly rectangular in shape, with jagged edges that looked like they had been torn from a larger piece. The stamp was a deep shade of blue, with a golden border that sparkled in the light .In the center of the stamp was a detailed illustration of the island, with palm trees, sandy beaches, and crystal clear water. The island was called Lost Lagoon, and according to the stamp, it was located just off the coast of the small town of Millvill. The stamp also had a series of mysterious symbols and writing on it that Sathivk and his friends couldn't decipher. They wondered what secrets the island might hold, and they were determined to find out. As they examined the stamp, they couldn't help but feel a sense of excitement and adventure. They knew that they had to go to Lost Lagoon and see what mysteries it held for themselves.

Sathivk: "Ok, so we have a stamp that leads to Lost Lagoon, an island full of hidden treasures and adventures. Now we just need a plan to get there."

Eoghan: "I know! We can build a boat and sail there ourselves."

Siuna : "Uh, I don't think we have the skills or materials to build a boat that can survive a journey to an island.

James: "I know! We can ask Grandpa to build us a boat. He's really good at building things."
Charlie: "That's a great idea! And he can be the captain of the boat too."

Sathivk: "Ok, let's go ask Grandpa. But we'll need to make sure we have all the supplies we need, like food, water, a map, and a satellite phone in case of an emergency."
Eoghan: "And don't forget the pirate hats and swords for the treasure hunt!"

Sathvik: "Right. Let's go see Grandpa and get started on our adventure to Lost Lagoon!"

14

Sathvik tiptoed into his grandpa's room, trying not to wake him up. But as he crept closer, he tripped over a pile of books and crashed to the floor with a loud thud.

Grandpa: (groggily) Wha...what is it, Sathivk?

Sathvik: we just found a stamp that led us to an island called Lost Lagoon!

Grandpa: (sitting up in bed) Lost Lagoon? I've never heard of it.

Sathvik: Yeah, I know! That's what makes it so exciting!

Grandpa: (rubbing his eyes) A treasure? This is all very interesting, but could you give me a minute to wake up?

Sathvik: Sorry, Grandpa. I'm just so excited!

Grandpa: (getting out of bed) It's okay, Sathvik. Let me take a look at this stamp. (He rummages through a drawer and pulls out an old map and a pair of glasses)

Sathvik: Here, let me help you. (He points to a spot on the map) It's right here, see? Lost Lagoon.

Grand pa runs his finger down the page

Yes, here it is. It's a small island just off the coast of Millvill.

Sathivk: Wow, I can't believe it! We really did find a mystery island!

Grandpa: Yes, it seems you did. And a treasure, too! This is quite an adventure you've had.
Sathivk: Can you help us build boat to get there

Grandpa had always been a bit of a handyman, and he loved nothing more than a good building project. So when Sathvik and his friends came to him with their plan to journey to Lost Lagoon, he knew exactly what to do.

He set to work building the boat, using leftover wood and scraps from around the garage. It wasn't the prettiest boat in the world, but it was sturdy and strong, and Grandpa knew it would get the job done.

He named the boat The Admiral's Ark, after the grand adventures he had always dreamed of having. And as he worked, he couldn't help but imagine all the exciting places the boat would take them.

"The Admiral's Ark" that Grandpa and Sathvik's friends built was quite a sight to behold. It was made out of a mishmash of materials, including leftover wood from a campfire, patches of canvas, and, of course, plenty of duct tape.

Despite its shoddy appearance, the boat was surprisingly sturdy and seaworthy. It had a small cabin for sleeping, a tiny kitchen for cooking,

Sathivk, Siuna , Eoghan, James, charlie, and Grandpa set off on their journey to Lost Lagoon in a rickety old boat The Admiral's ARK , that Grandpa had built.

As they sailed away from Milvill Town, they were filled with excitement and a sense of adventure. The journey was not without its humorous moments,

Grandpa had brought along his old sea captain's hat and hook hand, which he wore with pride as he navigated the boat. The kids couldn't stop laughing at his silly getup.

As they sailed further out to sea, the group also had to contend with the constant bickering of Eoghan and James, who couldn't seem to agree on anything. Despite the challenges and arguments, Sathivk and his friends were determined to reach Lost Lagoon. They sang sea shanties and played games to pass the time, dreaming of the treasure and adventures that awaited them on the mysterious island.

Finally, after what seemed like an eternity, the group arrived at Lost Lagoon.

Lost Lagoon was a small, tropical island that was shrouded in mystery. It was surrounded by crystal clear waters and pristine white sand beaches .The Island was covered in dense jungle, with tall trees and exotic plants everywhere. There were hidden coves and waterfalls to explore, as well as ancient ruins and abandoned temples. Rumor had it that Lost Lagoon was home to a treasure that had been hidden away by pirates long ago. Some said it was a chest full of gold and jewels, while others claimed it was a map to an even greater treasure.Regardless of the treasure's true nature, one thing was for sure: Lost Lagoon was a place of adventure and excitement, and Sathvik and his friends were eager to explore every inch of it.

Sathvik: "Look, Siuna! We're here! We made it to Lost Lagoon!"

Siuna: "Wow, it's even more beautiful than I imagined. Look at all those palm trees and crystal clear water."

Sathvik: "And check out that jungle! I bet there are all sorts of secrets and adventures hidden in there."

Siuna: "We should start searching for clues right away. The stamp said there was a treasure here, and we have to find it before anyone else does."

Eoghan: "Hey, don't forget about us! James, Charlie, and I will set up camp while you two go treasure hunting."

James: "Yeah and we'll even let Grandpa take a nap in the boat if he wants."

Grandpa: "Ah, that sounds like a fine idea. I could use a little rest after that boat journey. You kids go have fun and find that treasure."

Sathvik: "Thanks, Grandpa. We'll be back soon with the treasure in hand."

Siuna: "Come on, Sathvik. Let's go explore this island and see what secrets it holds."

Together, Sathvik and Siuna set off into the jungle, determined to find the treasure of Lost Lagoon.

Eoghan: "Ugh, I can't believe we have to set up camp in this jungle. It's so humid and buggy."

James: "Tell me about it. I'm already covered in sweat and mosquito bites."

Charlie : "At least we have Grandpa to help us. He's a pro at this kind of stuff."

Eoghan: "Yeah, but he's been snoring away in the boat for the past hour. I don't think he's going to be much help."

James: "Well, I guess we'll just have to figure it out on our own. Where do you want the tent, Eoghan?"

Eoghan: "I don't know, maybe over there near that big tree? But watch out for those vines, they're all tangled up."

Charlie : "What about the fire pit? Should we put it in the middle of camp or off to the side?"

James: "I don't know how about we just throw all the firewood in a heap and call it a day?"

Eoghan: "Very funny, James. We have to at least try to make this look like a proper campsite."

Just then, Grandpa emerged from the boat, rubbing his eyes. "What's all this commotion about? I was having the most delightful nap."

Eoghan: "Oh, Grandpa, thank goodness you're awake. We were trying to set up camp but we're having a bit of trouble."

Grandpa: "Well, don't worry, boys. I'll lend a hand. It's not every day that we get to go on a tropical adventure like this."

With Grandpa's help, Eoghan, James, and Charlie were able to set up a proper campsite on Lost Lagoon

Grandpa had definitely outdone himself when it came to setting up camp on Lost Lagoon. The tent was pitched in a clearing surrounded by palm trees, with a view of the ocean in the distance. The fire pit was expertly built, with a ring of stones and a stack of dry wood ready to be lit. Eoghan, James, and Charlie had done their best to help, but it was clear that Grandpa was the true master of campsite construction. He had even brought a few creature comforts from home, such as a small rocking chair to sit.

On the other side of the Island, Sathvik and Siuna set off into the jungle, following the map and searching for clues. After what felt like hours of searching,

they finally stumbled upon a hidden cave.

Siuna: "Sathvik, look! I found something!"

Sathvik: "What is it? A clue to the treasure?"

Siuna: "I think so! It's a map of the island, and there's an X marked on it."

Sathvik: "That must be where the treasure is hidden! Let's go find it!"

Siuna: "Wait, there's more. Look at the bottom of the map. It says 'In memory of King Villorthon, founder of Millvill and ruler of Lost Lagoon.' Do you think this treasure belongs to the king?"

Sathivk: "I don't know, but we have to find out. Come on, let's follow the map and see where it leads us."

Sathivk: "Look, Siuna! This must be it! The treasure must be inside!"

Siuna: "I can't believe it! We found it!"

The two of them rushed into the cave, and what they saw took their breath away. The cave was filled with gold coins, jewels, and ancient artifacts. It was like something out of a pirate movie. As Sathvik and Siuna entered the cave, they were greeted by a sight unlike anything they had ever seen before. The walls of the cave were lined with gold coins, sparkling jewels, and ancient artifacts. It was like something out of a fairy tale. Siuna couldn't believe her eyes. "Is this really happening? Are we actually seeing a real treasure cave?"

Sathvik was equally amazed. "I don't know, but I think we should take a closer look. Maybe we'll find a clue about who this treasure belongs to." As they made their way deeper into the cave, they saw a stone pedestal in the center of the room. On top of it was an old, ornate chest.

Sathivk approached the chest cautiously, unsure of what he would find inside. He slowly lifted the lid and gasped in amazement. The chest was filled to the brim with glittering jewels and sparkling gold coins.

Siuna couldn't contain her excitement. "Oh my gosh, Sathivk, we're rich! We're actually rich!"

Sathivk couldn't believe it. He had never seen so much wealth in his entire life. "This must be the treasure of King Villorthon. We have to tell Eoghan, James, Charlie, and Grandpa. They'll never believe it!"

Together, Sathivk and Siuna made their way back to camp, ready to share their incredible discovery with their friends. Sathivk and Siuna eagerly told their friends all about the   treasure cave

Eoghan: "That's amazing! I can't believe you guys actually found a real treasure."

James: "We have to see it for ourselves. Let's go back to the cave right now."

Siuna: "Definitely. We have to take some of the treasure back with us and show it to the people of Millvill."

Charlie: "Yeah, we should bring it to the town's history museum. They'll know what to do with it."

Grandpa: "I agree. It's important that the treasure is shared and appreciated .
Let's go back to the cave and gather as much as we can carry."

As they made their way back to the cave, they were all filled with excitement and anticipation. When they arrived, they couldn't believe their eyes. The cave was even more incredible than they had remembered, filled with sparkling jewels and glittering gold coins.

Together, they gathered up as much treasure as they could carry and made their way back to the boat. They couldn't wait to show the people of Millvill the amazing discovery they had made on Lost Lagoon.

Grandpa pulled out the satellite phone and dialed the mayor's number. As they waited for the mayor to pick up, the friends all crowded around, excited to share their news.

Grandpa: "Hello, Mayor. It's me, Sathivk's grandpa. We're on our way back to Millvill now and we have some exciting news to share with you."

Mayor: "What is it? Is everything alright?"

Grandpa: "Everything's fine. We've found a treasure cave on Lost Lagoon. It's filled with jewels and gold coins."

Mayor: "That's incredible! How did you find it?"

Sathvik : "We found a stamp and then a map and used our wits.

It was a real adventure."

Eoghan: "Yeah, and we had to work together as a team. It was a lot of fun."

Charlie: "We brought back as much treasure as we could carry. We thought it should be shared with the people of Millvill."

James: "We were thinking it could go in the town's history museum.

It's a really special find."

Mayor: "I agree. This is a truly remarkable discovery. Thank you for bringing it to our attention. We'll make sure it's properly displayed and appreciated."

As they hung up the phone, the friends all cheered and hugged each other in celebration.

After their amazing adventure on Lost Lagoon, Sathivk and his friends were hailed as heroes in the small town of Millvill.

The treasure they had found was placed in the town's history museum, where it was admired by all who came to see it.

But that wasn't the only thing that was put on display. The boat "The Admiral's Ark" that Grandpa had built was also placed in the museum, as a testament to the resourcefulness and ingenuity of the young treasure hunters.

Many people came to see The Admiral's Ark and hear the story of how it had been built from leftover wood and used to transport the friends to the distant island. The boat became a beloved attraction at the museum, and the friends were proud to have contributed something special to their community.

Sathivk and his friends were thrilled with the way their adventure had turned out. They had found a treasure, and learned valuable lessons about teamwork and perseverance. And they knew that they would always be remembered in the town of Millvill as the brave young adventurers who braved the dangers of Lost Lagoon to bring back a piece of history.

CHAPTER 2
SOAKED SAFARI

The Soaked Safari

 It was a scorching hot summer in the small town of Millville. The sun blazed down from the cloudless sky, turning the streets into shimmering ribbons of heat. The air was thick and sticky, and every surface seemed to sweat. The town's residents tried to find ways to stay cool. Some people set up sprinklers in their yards and ran through them in their swimsuits. Others lounged in the shade of trees or on the porches of their houses, sipping iced drinks and fanning themselves with newspapers. But the heat was unrelenting. Even the bravest ice cream eaters had to retreat inside, their brain freeze no match for the summer sun.

Sathivk and his friends hanging at Club house and the heat is killing them, and Suddenly
Eoghan was stuck with a paper flyer with big name on it as BEAT THE HEAT with a visit to
THE SOAKED SAFARI -

The new Water Theme Park in the Milvill Town .

The Soaked Safari in the small town of Millville was a sight to behold. It was a wild and wacky place, filled with all sorts of watery wonders. There was a giant slide that twisted and turned like a rollercoaster, spraying water on everyone who rode it. There was a lazy river that meandered through the park, allowing people to float along on inner tubes and soak up the sun. And there was a huge wave pool, where huge waves crashed down every few minutes, sending people tumbling and splashing. But the real draw of the water park was the "Splash Mountain" - a towering structure with multiple slides and waterfalls. People lined up for hours to ride it, screaming and laughing as they plunged down the steep drops and shot through the water.

Eoghan: Oh man, I've been dying to go to that place. I heard it has the biggest water slide in the whole county!

Charlie: Yeah, and I heard they have a giant wave pool too. I can't wait to get tossed around in the waves!

James: Me neither! And I heard they have a lazy river where you can just float around and relax in an inner tube. That sounds like the perfect way to beat the summer heat.

Siuna: Oh my gosh, I can't wait to go! It sounds like so much fun.

Sathvik: So, who's in for a trip to the Soaked Safari now ?

Eoghan: Count me in!

Charlie: Same here!

James: Me three!

Siuna: And me four!

The Gang took off to Soaked Safari , Sathvik and his friends, Charlie, James, Eoghan, and Sunia, were determined to have a great time at the water park When they arrived at The Soaked Safari, they were disappointed to find that the line was impossibly long. They waited and waited, but it seemed like they were never going to get in.

Just when they were about to give up hope, a park employee came over and told them that the park was at full capacity and they wouldn't be able to get in. Sathvik and his friends were devastated.

Siuna: Ugh, I can't believe we didn't get into The Soaked Safari.

Charlie: I know, right? The line was insane. We must have waited for hours.

James: Yeah, and then when we finally got to the front of the line, they told us that the park was at capacity and we couldn't get in.

Eoghan: This is ridiculous. We came all this way for nothing.

Sathvik : Don't worry guys, we'll just have to come up with Plan B.

Siuna: Plan B? What's Plan B?

Sathvik: We build our own water park in my backyard!

Siuna: Wow, that's a great idea! We could have a giant slide, a wave pool, and a lazy river.

Charlie: And we could have tropical drinks and cute lifeguards!

James: And we could charge admission and make a fortune!

Sathvik: Let's do it! The Soaked Safari has nothing on us!

Siuna: Yeah, we'll show them what a real water park looks like!

Sathvik and his friends were determined to have the best water park in town, and they were willing to do whatever it took to make it happen.

They spent hours in Sathvik's backyard, brainstorming ideas and coming up with creative solutions to the challenges they faced. They built a giant slide out of cardboard boxes and plastic sheeting, and they dug a wave pool in the dirt with shovels and buckets.

Sathvik: Okay, but we still need to figure out how to bring water to our water park. Any ideas?

Charlie: We could use a hose, but that would be kind of boring.

James: Yeah, we need something more epic.

Eoghan: I know! We could make artificial clouds maker and make it rain!

Siuna: How are we going to do that?

Eoghan: I saw it on a science show once. We just need to mix some dry ice and hot water, and it will create a cloud.

Sathvik: That sounds like a great idea! Let's give it a try.

So, Sathvik and his friends set to work creating their artificial clouds. They mixed the dry ice and hot water, and waited anxiously as a small cloud began to form. But things didn't go quite as planned. The cloud grew and grew, until it was a massive, swirling mass of vapor. And before they knew it, it began to rain - not just in Sathvik's backyard, but all over the town of Millville! Sathvik and his friends were shocked as they watched the town get drenched in water. They had never meant to cause such a commotion,

Sathvik: Oh no, what have we done? The whole town is flooded!

Charlie: We didn't mean to cause such a commotion. We were just trying to make it rain for our water park.

James: Yeah, but we never expected it to be so intense.

Eoghan: We have to do something to fix this.

Siuna: I know! We can ask Sathvik's grandparents for help. They always know what to do in a crisis.

Sathvik: Great idea! I'll go call them right now.

Sathvik: Grandpa, Grandma, we need your help!
The whole town is flooded and it's all our fault.
Grandpa: What happened, Sathvik?
Sathvik: We were trying to build a water park in my backyard, and we thought it would be cool to make it rain. So, we made an artificial cloud, but things got out of control and the whole town got drenched.
Grandma: Oh my. Well, don't worry, we'll fix this. Your grandpa and I have faced bigger challenges in our time.
Sathvik : Really ? !!
Grandma: Okay, we need to come up with a plan to save the town from these floods.
Grandpa: I've got an idea. We'll use my special flood-fighting machine !!! .

Grandpa: "we've got the old washing machine motor, the vacuum cleaner hose, and a bunch of PVC pipes. Think we can make a flood fighting machine out of this?"

Grandma: "Well, we've got to make do with what we've got. But I think we can make something that'll pump out the water at least."

Grandpa: "That's the spirit! Now, I was thinking we could use the PVC pipes as the main body of the machine, and attach the hose to the end for the water to flow out of."

Grandma: "And what about the motor? How are we going to power this thing?"

Grandpa: "That's where the washing machine motor comes in. We'll rig it up to a generator and voila! We've got ourselves a flood fighting machine."

Grandma: "Well, it's not the most conventional design, but I trust your engineering skills. Let's get to work!"

Grandpa: "This is going to be a work of art, you'll see. We'll call it the "Flood-Buster 3000" and we'll be the heros of the town."

And the gang used the flood- fighting Machine at every house and pump of the town. Sathvik's grandma, a master cook, put her culinary skills to use by cooking up a batch of her famous hot cocoa for everyone to enjoy while they waited for the water to recede.

Sathvik: I can't believe we caused such a mess. The whole town is flooded!

Charlie: Yeah, but at least we have your grandparents to help us fix things.

James: They're like superheroes or something.

Eoghan: Yeah, I don't know what we would do without them.

Siuna: I'm just glad everyone is okay.

Sathvik: Me too. I'm sorry we caused so much trouble.

Grandpa: Don't worry, Sathvik. Accidents happen. The important thing is that we were able to fix things and everyone is safe.

Grandma: That's right. And we had a lot of fun doing it. I haven't had this much excitement in a long time.

Sathvik: I'm glad you enjoyed it, Grandma. But I think we should probably stick to less intense activities from now on.

Grandpa: I think that's a good idea. You kids have plenty of time for excitement as you grow older.

Grandma: And we'll always be here to help out when you need us.

Sathvik: Thanks, Grandma. Thanks, Grandpa. You guys are the best.

Sathvik and his friends were grateful to have such wonderful grandparents, and they were relieved that the town was saved. They knew that they had learned a valuable lesson about the importance of being careful with their experiments, and they were determined to be more responsible in the future.

CHAPTER 3
HAIR MAN

Hair Man

Sathvik and his friends, are all huge fans of comics and they love spending their time, after school at the local comic book store, "The Comic Kingdom".

"The Comic Kingdom" is a small, but cozy comic book store located in the heart of Millvill. It's known for its wide selection of comics and graphic novels, ranging from the latest superhero blockbusters to independent and alternative comics. The store is decorated with colorful posters, action figures, and other comic-related merchandise that gives it a fun and inviting atmosphere.

The store is run by Mr. Johnson, an older man who has been a fan of comics his whole life. He is a friendly and knowledgeable owner who is always happy to chat with customers about the latest comics and help them find new favorites. He is a great storyteller and often shares stories about his days as a comic book seller and his own personal experience reading comics. He has a lot of knowledge about comics and is passionate about sharing it with his customers. Even though the store is small, it has a big heart and it's a vital part of the local community and loved by people of all ages.

Sathvik and the Gang, often hang out at the store, browsing through the latest issues, chatting with the owner, Mr. Johnson and other customers who share their passion for comics.

It's not only a store for them, but it's a second home, a place where they can be themselves and discuss about the comics and characters they love. They are always excited to discover new comics and share their thoughts with each other.

Sathvik: "Hey guys, check out this new issue of 'Superhero Squad'! It has a giant robot on the cover and it looks amazing!"

Charlie: "Wow, that robot is huge! I bet it can crush cities with one hand."

Suina: "Yeah, but I bet it can't dance. I heard that the new villain in 'Dancing Divas' can turn her enemies into disco zombies."

Eoghan: "Disco Zombies? That's ridiculous! What kind of superpower is that?"

James: "I heard that the new comic book series 'Mystery Mansion' is coming out soon and it's going to be a hit. Have you guys read it yet?"

Charlie: "Interesting? It's the most intriguing and mysterious comic book series I've ever read!"

Suddenly Sathvik sees the 90% sale , Closing down sale .
(Sathvik and his friends approaches Mr Johnson)

Sathvik: "Hey Mr. Johnson, what's with the 90% off sale? Is everything okay?"

Mr. Johnson: "I'm afraid not, Sathvik. I've decided to close the store. Business has been slow and I can't afford to keep it running any longer."

Sathvik: "What? But why? This store is like a second home to me and my friends."

Mr. Johnson: "I know, Sathvik. It's been a tough decision to make, but it's just not financially viable for me to keep the store open. I'm having a sale to try and clear out my inventory before I close."

Sathvik: "But, where will I and my friends buy comics now? and what will we do without a store? We're used to come here and hang out after school and talk about comics."

Mr. Johnson: "I know it's hard, Sathvik. I'm going to miss this place just as much as you and your friends will. But you can still read comics and have conversations about them with your friends, just in different places."

Sathvik: "I know you're right Mr. Johnson, it's just hard to imagine not having this store and you here. But we'll find a way to keep reading comics and hang out together. Thank you for everything"

Sathvik: "Okay, so we need to come up with a plan to save the store. Any ideas?"

Charlie: "We could organize a fundraising event, like a bake sale or a car wash."

James: "That's a great idea, but I think we need something , which can save the store and get people back to buy more comics "

Sathvik: "I know! We could create our own comic book series and sell it at the store.

Charlie: "That's a fantastic idea! But what should our comic book series be about?"

Suina : "I know! We could make a comic book series about a superhero with hair-powers! We could call it 'Hair Man'!" , like your Hair Sathvik !!

Eoghan: "That's perfect! We could make it a comical and funny comic book series for kids like us. It will be a hit!"

Sathvik: "Let's do it! We'll create 'Hair Man' and save the store with our own comic book series."

Hair Man

Volume -01

Story & Illustrations by : Nuts and Bolts Club

one Day

A boy was walking near a Chemical Factory

He Tripped on a can and ...

He fell in Radio Active X water in the Factory ...

Some where in the same town there was a evil Barber called ... Dr Scissors

Dr. Scissors is a villainous hairdresser who is the archenemy of Hair Man

he has a secret door, in his shop

it opens to a EVIL LAB, Dr Scissors, wanted to steal Hairman powers and take over the Universe.

Dr. Scissors, was working on his evil plan ....

Dr.Scissors, comes up with a brillant plan to attack Hair Man

The Scissor's soon march through the city, causing chaos and destruction. Buildings are crumbling, cars are overturned,

Dr.Scissors, attacks the town with his army of The Scissors

Quickly Hair Man , uses his powers to destroy DR.Scissors

DR.Scissors, Sees that his army is destroyed, He Escapes in his helicopter

Hair Man stands victorious, but with a look of determination,
knowing that Dr. Scissors will surely return with a new plan.

After finishing the "Hair Man" the comic book, the gang are excited to share their
story with the world. They decide to approach their grandparents for support in
getting the comic book published.

Sathvik: "Grandma, Grandpa, we have something we want to show you."

Grandma: "Oh, what is it dear?"

Grandpa: "Let's see it, my grandkids never cease to amaze me"

Charlie: "We created a comic book called 'Hair Man' and we want to get it published."

Siuna: "It's about a boy who gets superpowers after falling in a puddle of radioactive X and uses them to stop the evil Dr Scissors"

Grandpa and Grandma Reads the book and they love it.

Grandpa: "You know what, I know a friend of mine "MR, Ronaldo Books" who is a very wealthy man and has a soft spot for comics and kids, let me give him a call"

Eoghan: "That would be great, Grandpa! We really think our comic book has the potential to be a hit."

James: "Yeah, we worked really hard on it and we think it could help save the comic book store"

Grandpa: "I'll call him right now, hold on"

Grandpa: "Hi, old friend! How's it going?"

Mr Ronaldo Books,: "Oh, hey there! Not too bad, just making more money. How about you?"

Grandpa: "I'm doing well too, thanks for asking. Listen, I've got something I want to run by you. My grandkids just created a comic book series called 'Hair Man' and they're trying to get it published."

Mr. Ronaldo Books: "Oh, that sounds interesting. What's it about?"

Grandpa: "It's about a boy who gets superpowers after falling in a puddle of radioactive X and uses them to stop the evil Dr Scissors"

Mr. Ronaldo Books: "Hahaha! that's sounds hilarious. I love comics and kids, send me the comic book and I'll have a look"

Grandpa: "Great! They're really excited about it and they're hoping to save a local comic book store by publishing their comics"

Mr. Ronaldo Books: "That's a great cause. If the comic book is good, I'll publish it and we'll save the comic book store together. I'll be there in an hour"

Grandpa: "Thank you, I knew I could count on you. You're always been the best friend"

Mr. Ronaldo Books: "Anything for you, old buddy"

"HairMan" comic book series quickly became a sensation after it was published, with the story and characters resonating with readers of all ages. The comic book's unique story about a boy who trips and falls in radioactive X, giving him superpowers and the task of saving the world from a villainous hairdresser, Dr. Scissors,

The comic book quickly became a best-seller, with strong sales numbers and rave reviews from critics and readers alike. The comic book series was so popular that it became a hit overnight, and it generated enough money to save the local comic book store, which was on the verge of closing.

The store went from being in danger of closing to becoming a thriving business, with a steady stream of customers coming in to buy the latest issues of "Hair Man" and other comics..

Sathvik: "Guys, can you believe it? Our comic book 'Hair Man' is a hit! We've earned enough money to save the comic book store!"

Charlie: "I knew it would be a success! The story of Hair Man tripping in radio X and getting super powers was a genius idea!"

Eoghan: "Yeah, I never thought I'd enjoy wearing a Hair Man t-shirt so much, but it was all worth it"

Sathvik: "Me too! And the best part is, we get to keep going to the comic book store and buying all the comics we want"

Charlie: "That's right, no more 90% off sales! The store is here to stay"

Sathvik: "Anything is possible, with our Nuts and Bolts Club"

CHAPTER 4
THE BIG FOOT

The Bigfoot

Sathvik's grandparents want to surprise the kids with a fun-filled trip to the woods in a rented camper van. They plan to take the kids on a two-day adventure where they can explore the great outdoors, go camping and make new memories together. The kids are excited about the trip and can't wait to hit the road in the retro camper van and see what the woods have in store for them.

Sathivk: "Grandpa, this camper van is amazing! I can't believe we get to go on a camping trip in it!"

Grandpa: "I'm glad you like it, Sathivk. Your grandmother and I used to go on road trips all the time when we were young."

Sathivk: "Really? That sounds like so much fun!"

Grandma: "Just make sure we all stay together and be careful out there, okay?"

Sathivk: "Don't worry, Grandma. We'll be safe. And who knows, we might even discover something amazing!"

Grandpa: "Like what? Aliens? (laughing) "

Sathivk: "You never know, Grandpa. You never know."

Grandma: "Just be safe, and Lets have fun!"

Sathivk: "We will, Grandma. Don't worry. We're the Nuts and Bolts club, we can handle anything!"

The camper van was an old retro-style vehicle with a bright orange paint job and a white roof. The interior was cozy and compact, with a small kitchenette and seating that converted into beds for sleeping. The gang was excited as they climbed inside, joking and laughing as they explored the different features of the van. The windows were large and offered a great view of the passing scenery. The camper van was equipped with all the amenities they needed for their trip to the woods, including a small stove, refrigerator, and sink. The gang was in high spirits as they set off on their adventure, looking forward to the fun and excitement that lay ahead.

As Sathvik and his friends climb into the rented camper van, they can't help but admire its retro design. "Wow, this is so cool!" exclaims Charlie. "It's like we're traveling back in time!" Eoghan agrees, "I've never been in a camper van before, this is going to be an adventure!" Siuna, looks around nervously. "I hope it's clean," she says, "I don't want to catch any germs." James, who is the most outgoing of the group, starts exploring the van, "Look, there's a little kitchen and a table, we can play cards and eat snacks while we're on the road." Sathvik's grandpa, who is the one who rented the van, chuckles. "That's the idea, kiddos," he says, "We're going to have a blast!"

As the gang and Sathvik's grandparents set off on their journey to the woods, they were filled with excitement and anticipation. The camper van was cozy and had all the amenities they needed for their trip. They sang songs, played games and enjoyed the beautiful scenery as they drove through the winding roads leading to the woods. The grandparents regaled the kids with stories of their own camping trips from when they were young. The kids were fascinated by the tales of campfires, roasting marshmallows and exploring the great outdoors. As they reached the woods, the gang was eager to set up camp and explore the wilderness.

As the camper van pulled up to the woods, Sathvik and his friends couldn't contain their excitement. They jumped out of the van and immediately started exploring their surroundings. Meanwhile, sathvik's grandpa and grandma set about preparing the campground. Grandpa, who had spent many years in the army, set up the tent with military precision. The gang, eager to help out, offered to pitch in. Charlie, , helped Grandpa with the tent. Eoghan, set up the portable camping stove. James and Siuna, who were both animal lovers, went to explore the woods to look for kindling.

Sathvik: "Grandma, can I gather some sticks for the fire?"

Grandma: "Of course, dear. Just be careful not to step on any poison ivy."

Siuna: "I found some berries! Can we make a pie with them?"

Grandma: "That sounds delicious! We'll have to see if they're safe to eat first."

Charlie: "I can't believe we're camping in a camper van! It's like the best of both worlds!"

Grandpa: "Yes, I thought it would be a nice change from the usual camping in a tent."

James: "I brought my portable charger, so we can charge our phones while we're in the woods."

Eoghan: "What's the point of that? We're here to enjoy nature, not stare at screens."

As they set up camp and settled in for the night, they couldn't help but feel a sense of excitement and adventure.

As the group settled down for the night in their camp site, they started to hear strange noises coming from the woods. Sathvik, Eoghan, James, and Charlie were intrigued and wanted to investigate, but Grandpa cautioned them to be careful. "It's probably just an animal," he said, "but we should still be careful."

"I'm coming with you!" said Siuna, excitedly.

"No, no, no," said Grandma, "You stay here with me. We'll make some hot cocoa and you can tell me all about your adventures."

"But Grandma, I want to see what is that !" complained Siuna.

Grand ma and siuna stayed back at camp. And rest are off to the wild.

As they walked into the woods, Grandpa leading the way with a flashlight in one hand and a stick in the other, ready to defend them from any wild animals.
As they walked deeper into the woods, the noises grew louder and the group grew more excited. Suddenly, they saw a figure in the distance. "Is that it? Is that the bear?" whispered Sathvik.

"I don't know, let's go find out," said Grandpa, leading the way.

As they got closer, they realized that it was not a bear, but an injured bigfoot

Grandpa: "What in tarnation is that thing?"
Sathvik: "I think it's a bigfoot!"
Charlie: "No way, I thought they were just legends!"
Eoghan: "It looks hurt, we have to help it!"
Grandpa: "Well I'll be, it is a bigfoot! And it looks like it needs our help."
Sathvik: "But what do we do? We can't just leave it here."
Grandpa: "We'll call the wildlife rescue in the morning, but for now we'll make sure it's comfortable and keep an eye on it."

The creature was covered in thick, dark fur and had large, powerful-looking feet.
It appeared to be injured, with a gash on its leg and a look of pain on its face.

"We have to help it," Grandpa said, as he carefully approached the creature.

The gang was amazed, but also a bit scared.

Meanwhile, Eoghan and James were trying to decide on a name for the big foot.

Eoghan: "How about Biggy? It's a fitting name for such a big creature."

James: "No way, that's too boring. We need something more catchy, like Sasquatch."

Eoghan: "Sasquatch? That sounds like a brand of shampoo."

James: "Well, it's better than Biggy. Plus, it's a classic name for a bigfoot."

Eoghan: "Hmm, I guess you have a point. But I still think we should come up with something more unique."

James: "How about Bobo? It's short, sweet, and catchy."

Eoghan: "Bobo? That sounds like a clown's name. I don't think that's fitting for a mythical creature."

Sathvik: "Guys,, Will you both please stop it !! We'll come up with something better. For now, let's just focus on getting that bigfoot some help."

Eoghan: "Agreed. Let's get back to the camp and tell the others what we found."

The Group, returned to camp to meet Grandma and Siuna

Sathvik: "Guys, you won't believe what we just found in the woods!"

Suina: "A treasure chest? A hidden cave? Aliens?"

Eoghan: "No, something even better! We found a bigfoot!"

Grandma: "You're kidding me, right?"

Sathvik: "I wish we were! But it's true, we saw it with our own eyes. But the poor thing is injured."

Siuna: "Oh my gosh, that's amazing! But what are we going to do to help it?"

Grandpa explains the details of the Bigfoot,

Grandma: "I think we should call Dr. Raj, he's the town vet. He'll know what to do."

Grandpa: "Good idea, I'll call him right now."

Sathvik: "But we have to make sure we keep this a secret. We don't want the whole town to know, it could put the bigfoot in danger."

Charlie: "Yeah, we don't want to be famous for finding a bigfoot and then it getting hurt because of us."

Grandma: "I agree, we'll keep it between us for now. But first, let's get that bigfoot some help."

Raj arrived at the camp early next morning and was greeted by the excited faces of
athvik, Eoghan, James, Charlie and Siuna. He couldn't believe his eyes when they led
m to the injured Bigfoot.

e immediately got to work, checking the bigfoot's vital signs and assessing its injuries.

"Wow, I've never seen anything like this before!" said Dr Raj in amazement.
"We know, we were pretty surprised ourselves," said Sathvik with a chuckle.
"Well, we better get to work then. I need to clean these wounds and administer some painkillers," said Dr Raj as he opened his medical bag. "Can we help?" asked Eoghan eagerly. "Sure, you can help by keeping an eye on the Bigfoot's vital signs and making sure it stays calm," said Dr Raj. "This is amazing!" said James.

"I never thought I would get to see a real-life bigfoot up close." "Yeah, it's pretty cool," said Charlie. "But we have to make sure it gets back to the wild safely."

"That's right," said Dr Raj. "We need to make sure it's fully healed before we release it back into the wild."

After the treatment, the Bigfoot was healed and ready to go back to the wild. The gang and Dr. Raj carefully released the bigfoot back into the woods, and as it walked away, it left behind a token of its visit in the form of a large footprint

 The gang was overjoyed that they were able to help the bigfoot, but they were a bit disappointed that they didn't get to take a picture of it. Grandpa then comforted the kids, saying that they should be happy they were able to help the bigfoot and that the footprint would always be a reminder of their adventure.

The kids laughed and agreed and they continued to kept the secret of bigfoot for rest of their lives.

CHAPTER 5
THE KART'ASTROPHIC RACE

The Kart-astrophic Race

Sathvik and his gang were walking around the streets of Millvill when they stumbled upon a billboard advertising "The Cart King Cup". The race was open to kids under the age of 10 and the prize was a brand new cart. The gang was excited at the thought of participating in the race and building their own cart. They had never participated in the race before, but this year they were determined to give it a shot.

Later That afternoon ,The gang were hanging at Nuts & Bolts Club and ,,

Sathvik: "Guys, I've been thinking. We should participate in the CartKing Cup, this year."

Eoghan: "That's a great idea, Sathvik. But have you seen the competition? Gearville has won the past 15 years in a row."

Charlie: "Yeah, and they're known for their high-tech carts. How are we supposed to compete with that?"

Sathvik: "I know it'll be tough, but I'm confident we can build a cart that'll give them a run for their money."

James: "But where are we going to get the materials to build it? Our parents don't give us , the money to buy a fancy cart kit."

Siuna: "What about Grandpa and Grandma? They're always tinkering with stuff in the garage. Maybe they could help us out."

Sathvik: "That's a great idea, Siuna. But they're on vacation in Mount Everest right now. They won't be back for a couple of weeks."

Eoghan: "we can build one. We can use all the scrap materials,

Siuna: "That's a great idea, Eoghan! But where will we get the scrap materials from?"

Eoghan : we can go to the Town's Junkyard and ask for help from MR.Rusty McSrcap , I heard he is very good person.

Sathvik: "That's the spirit! Let's get to work and build the best cart in town for the CartKing Cup!"

Charlie: "Yeah, let's do it! We'll call ourselves the Scrappy Racers."

James: "Ha! I like that. The Scrappy Racers, ready to take on the CartKing Cup!"

Siuna: "Alright, let's gather all the materials and start building. We only have a few weeks until the race!"

Sathvik: "Let's get to work, team! The CartKing Cup awaits!"

Next Day they approached local junkyard, where they were greeted by the owner, who is well known as Mr. Rusty McScrap.

Sathvik: "Hi Mr. Rusty McScarap, we're a group of friends from Millvill Town and we're building a cart for the Annual CartKing Cup. We were wondering if you could help us out with some materials from your junkyard?"

Mr.Rusty McScarap: "Well, well, well. Look what we have here. A group of young inventors, huh? Tell me more about this cart you're building."

Sathvik: "We're using scrap materials to build it and we're trying to keep costs low. We're hoping to beat Gearville Town, who has won the past 15 years in a row."

Mr.Rusty McScarap: "I see. Well, I'll tell you what. I'll give you all the scrap materials you need, but in return, I want you to put my junkyard's logo on your cart."

Sathvik: "That's a great deal, Mr. Rusty. Thank you so much for your support."

Mr. Rusty: "why don't I give you a tour of the junkyard and you can pick out whatever materials you need?"

As Mr. Rusty gave the tour of the junkyard, the gang saw all kinds of scrap materials that could be useful for building their cart. Old bike wheels, spare metal, and even an old lawnmower engine.

Sathvik: "Wow, this is amazing Mr. Rusty. We're sure that we'll find everything we need here."

Mr. Rusty : "I'm glad you kids think so. And remember, if you need anything else, just let me know. I'll be happy to help you out."

Sathvik: "Thank you, Mr. Rusty. We really appreciate it."

Mr. Rusty: "No problem, kids. Good luck with your cart building and in the race. And let me know if you need any help with delivering the materials to your club house."

Sathvik and gang were excited to start working on their cart. They had gathered a lot of scrap materials from Mr. Rusty's junkyard, including old bike wheels, wood, and metal. They had also received some sponsorship from local stores to help cover the cost of other materials they needed.

They set up a workspace in the garage of Sathvik's grandparent's house and got to work. Sathvik took charge of the design and overall layout of the cart, while Eoghan worked on the frame and Charlie focused on the wheels. James and Siuna worked on the engine and electrical systems.

They spent hours working on the cart, fine-tuning every detail and making sure everything was perfect. They had a lot of fun working together and laughing at their mistakes. They also had a lot of questions and Mr Rusty was happy to help them with his knowledge and experience.

As they worked, they would step back and admire their progress, feeling proud of what they had accomplished so far. They knew they still had a long way to go, but they were determined to build the best cart in town and make Millvill proud.

Sathvik: "Alright, gang. We've finally finished building our cart. Now we need to give it a name."

Charlie: "How about 'The Scrapyard Speedster'?"

James: "I like 'The Junk Yard Jumper'."

Eoghan: "I think 'The Rusty Racer' has a nice ring to it."

Siuna: "I've got it! 'The Dumpster Dynamo'."

Sathvik: "I like that one, Siuna. It's catchy and fitting since we got most of the materials from Mr. Rusty's junkyard."

Charlie: "Yeah, and it also sounds powerful and fast."

James: "Agreed. 'The Dumpster Dynamo' it is."

THE DUMPSTER DYNAMO

Sathvik: "Guys, I've been thinking. We need to think about our pit stop team for the CartKing Cup."

Eoghan: "Yeah, the rules say we need a minimum of five people. We've got the four of us, but we're one short."

Sathvik: "Hey guys, I've got an idea for our pitstop team. How about we ask Caitlin to join us? She's fast and agile, and I think she'd be a great addition."

Eoghan: "Caitlin? My little sister? Are you sure about that, Sathvik?"

Charlie: "I don't know, Sathvik. She's just a kid. Can she really handle the pressure of a race like this?"

Sathvik: "I think she can. And honestly, I don't think we have many other options. We need at least five people on our pitstop team, and right now we only have four."

James: "Alright, I'm in. Let's give her a shot."

Siuna: "Me too. I think it'll be fun to have a girl on the team."

Eoghan: "I guess it couldn't hurt to ask. But you should know, Caitlin can be pretty demanding. She's going to want something in return for her help."

Sathvik: "we are prepared for that. "

Eoghan: "Ha! Good luck with that. ."

Sathvik: "Great. Let's go ask her now."

The gang all head over to Eoghan's house to ask Caitlin if she would be willing to join their pitstop team.

sathvik: "Caitlin, we really need your help with the pit stop. Are you in?"

Caitlin: "I don't know, I've never worked on a pit stop before. What do I have to do?"

Siuna: "It's pretty simple, you just have to change the wheels and refuel the cart. Plus, you're really fast and agile, so you'll be perfect for the job."

Caitlin: "Okay, I'll do it. But, I have one condition."

Sathvik: "What's that?"

Caitlin: "Free lifetime chocolate shakes at Forks and Fingers. Deal?"

Sathvik: "Deal! Thank you so much, Caitlin. You're a lifesaver."

Caitlin: "No problem. I'm just glad I can help. Let's win this thing!"

Siuna: "Alright, let's get to work and prepare for the race!"

The Dumpster Dynamo, was not reaching its maximum speed during test drives on the custom track built by Mr. Rusty. Sathvik and the gang were puzzled as to why this was the case. They had put in a lot of effort and time into building the car, but it seemed like something was holding it back. They would gather around the car after each test drive, trying to diagnose the problem. They would check the engine, the wheels, and the aerodynamics, but everything seemed to be in working order. They couldn't figure out what the issue was, and it was starting to become a source of frustration for the gang. They knew they had to fix the problem before the big race if they wanted to have any chance of winning.

Later that evening, Gang were back in Fork and Fingers , Disappointed that cart is not picking speed as expected

Sathvik: "Man, I can't believe our cart is still so slow. We've been working on it for weeks now."

Eoghan: "Yeah, I thought all the scrap materials we got from Mr. Rusty would make it go faster."

James: "Maybe we're missing something important. I wish Grandpa and Grandma were here to help us out."

Siuna: "Yeah, they're the experts when it comes to building things with scrap materials."

Conor: (overhearing the conversation) "Excuse me, but I couldn't help but overhear your conversation. I'm Conor, the new kid in town. I'm pretty good with mechanics and I might be able to help you out."

Sathvik: "Really? That would be great, Conor. We could use all the help we can get."

Conor: "First of all, you need to change the rubber on the wheels. It's not the right type for the kind of speed you're trying to reach."

Eoghan : "I never thought of that, Thanks Conor."

Conor : "No problem, I am happy to help.

Charlie : "You know what, let's give it a try and test it out in the junkyard."

Sathvik : "That's a great idea! Let's get to work and see if we can make Dumpster Dynamo the fastest cart in town."

Conor: "I'm excited to help you guys build the best cart in town."

With Conor's addition to the team, the gang practiced in the junk yard and the car was reaching high speeds. Sathvik was taking the drive, Eoghan leading the mechanics with Conor, and Siuna and Caitlin in charge of pitstops along with James and Charlie. The team was working together seamlessly, and the car was performing better than ever before. They were all excited to see how the car would perform in the race, and were determined to give Gearville Town a run for their money. With the help of Conor, the gang was able to fix the issue with the rubber and the car was able to reach the speed they were aiming for. They were all excited and ready for the big day of the race, and were sure that with the hard work and determination, they would be able to win the CartKing Cup.

The Day of the CartKing Cup Arrived, The crowd at the CartKing Cup is buzzing with excitement as the teams from all over the region gather to show off their homemade carts. The Gearville Town team is present with their high-tech cart, "The Gear Grinder", and the crowd cheers as it makes a lap around the track. But there's also a new team that has caught the attention of the crowd: the Millville team with their cart "Dumpster Dynamo" made from scrap materials. The crowd is curious to see how this underdog team will fare against the reigning champion Gearville. Other notable carts are "The Rust Bucket" from Rustyville, "The Junk Yard Dog" from Scrapyard City and "The Wrench Warriors" from Gearville. The announcer also mentions that the Millville team is the only one that is under 10 age group. The teams line up at the starting line, and the crowd holds its breath as the countdown begins. The race is about to begin and the tension is palpable as everyone waits for the starting gun to go off.

Sathvik: "Alright guys, we've worked hard for this. Let's show everyone what we're made of."

Eoghan: "I've got the tools ready, Sathvik. Just let me know if you need anything."

Charlie: "I've got the spare parts here, just in case something breaks."

James: "I've got the fuel and oil, we're good to go."

Siuna: "Caitlin and I are ready for the pit stops, just give us a signal."

Sathvik: "Alright, I'm getting in the driver's seat now. Wish me luck!"

Eoghan: "You don't need luck, Sathvik. You've got skill."

Charlie: "And a kick-ass cart."

James: "Don't forget the team behind you."

Siuna: "We've got your back, Sathvik. Let's do this!"

Sathvik: "Alright, here we go! Revving engine"

(As the race progresses)

Eoghan: "Sathvik, I need you to come in for a pit stop. We need to change the tires."

Sathvik: "Copy that, Eoghan. Caitlin, get ready!"

Caitlin: "On it, Sathvik!"

Siuna: "Tires changed, Sathvik. You're good to go!"

Sathvik: "Thanks, team! I'm back on the track!"

James: "Sathvik, we're seeing some smoke coming from the engine.
We need to bring you in for a check-up."

Sathvik: "Copy that, James. Conor, what's the problem?"

Conor: "It looks like a problem with the spark plugs. I'll fix it up in no time."

Sathvik: "Hurry, Conor. I don't want to lose too much time in the pit stop."

Conor: "Got it, Sathvik. Alright, all fixed. You're good to go."

Sathvik: "Thanks, Conor. Let's finish this race strong!"

As Sathvik approached the final lap, the tension in the pitstop was palpable. His friends were cheering him on, and he could feel the adrenaline pumping through his veins. He was in third place, just behind the cart from Gearville, the reigning champion for the past 15 years. Sathvik knew that this was his chance to make a move and secure second place.

Sathvik: "Guys, we're on the final lap! We're in third place and we're catching up to second!"

Eoghan: "Keep pushing, Sathvik! We can do this!"

Sathvik: "I see Gearville Town's cart up ahead. I'm going to try to pass them!"

James: "Be careful, Sathvik! They're known for their dirty tactics."

Sathvik: "I'm going for it! overtakes Gearville Town's cart I did it! We're in second place!"

Eoghan: "Great job, Sathvik! Now let's take first place!"

Charlie: "Wait, what's happening with Gearville Town's cart? It looks like they're losing control!"

James: "Oh no, they're going to crash!"

Siuna: "Sathvik, stop the cart! We have to help that kid!"

The Gearville cart had lost control and was skidding towards him. In that moment, Sathvik knew that he had to make a split-second decision. He could either try to avoid the collision and secure his own victory, or he could try to help the other cart and its driver.

Without hesitation, Sathvik turned his own cart towards the Gearville cart, trying to slow it down and prevent a crash. It was a desperate move, but it worked. The Gearville cart came to stop just inches away from his own. Sathvik and his gang rushed over to the other cart to check on the driver. It was a kid, no older than them. Sathvik and his friends helped the kid out of the cart .

There was silence every where . Sathvik had just lost the race.
The announcers were in shock and didn't know what to say, as the crowd erupted in
applause for Sathvik and his gang.
Announcer: "Ladies and gentlemen, what we just witnessed here was truly incredible.
Sathvik and his team were in the lead, just seconds away from winning the CartKing Cup,
when they made the selfless decision to stop and help a competitor who had been injured.
This is the true spirit of sportsmanship, and I am honored to be a part of this community
that values compassion and sportsmanship above winning at all costs."
Crowd: Applause

Announcer: "Sathvik and his team may have lost the Cup, but they have won the hearts of
everyone here today. Let's give them a round of applause."
Crowd: Standing ovation

Sathvik: "We may have lost the race, but we couldn't just stand by and watch someone get hurt. It's not about winning or losing, it's about doing the right thing."

Eoghan: "Yeah, and we're just glad that the other kid is okay."

Charlie: "And we'll always have the memory of this experience and the knowledge that we did the right thing."

Siuna: "Plus, free lifetime chocolate shakes at Fork and Fingers!"

James: "That's right! We may have lost the Cup, but we won something even more valuable: the respect and admiration of our community."

Crowd: Applause

Announcer: "Once again, let's give a round of applause for Sathvik and his team for their sportsmanship and compassion."

About Author

Meet Naveen Maremanda, the mastermind behind "world of Sathvik and his friends". Naveen, hailing from the bustling city of Hyderabad, India, is the son of Maremanda Seetha Ramaiah, well-known journalist in Indian newspapers, and Sita Ratna Kumari who is a home-making. From a young age, Naveen had a passion for storytelling and visual arts, leading him to start classical animation at the age of Ten.

During his college days, Naveen created animated children's stories and rhymes that were a huge hit in the early 2000s. Fast forward to now, Naveen is a successful software professional by day, but by night he transforms into a creative force, bringing to life the adventures of Sathvik and his gang through his writing.

But, where did Naveen get his inspiration for the character of Sathvik? Well, it's no coincidence that his own son is named Sathvik. That's right, Naveen's own little sidekick has been his inspiration all along!

When asked about the creation of the book, Naveen says, "I just wanted to write something that both kids and adults can enjoy. And also I wanted to thank my father, who always supported me in my passion for writing and my mother for always being there for me and my wife Vishnu Priya , for putting up with me when I was writing."

So there you have it, folks. Next time you're flipping through the pages of "The World of Sathvik and his Friends", just remember, it's all thanks to the wild imagination of Naveen Maremanda.

Printed in Great Britain
by Amazon

21263361R00066